MY SCOTTISH ~~ACTIVITY~~ leisure ACTIVITY BOOK

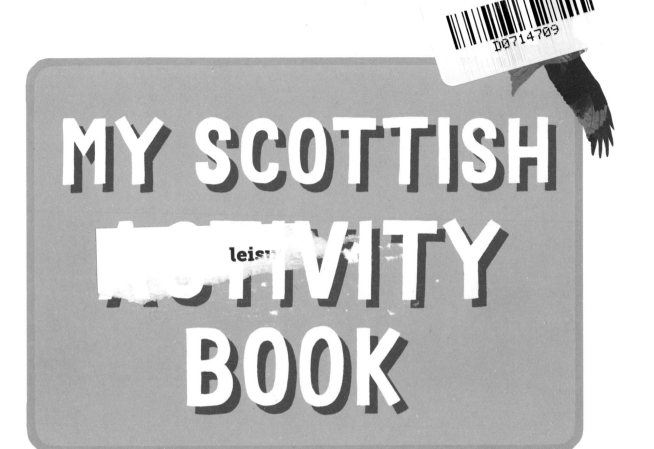

Author – Sasha Morton
Illustrator – Charlotte Pepper

BC

This edition published in 2020 by

BC Books, an imprint of
Birlinn Limited
West Newington House
10 Newington Road
Edinburgh EH9 1QS

www.birlinn.co.uk

Author: Sasha Morton
Illustrator: Charlotte Pepper

ISBN: 978-1-78027-652-6

Printed in India

Hello!
Welcome to My Scottish Activity Book.
Inside, you'll find lots of things to do,
ideas to explore and fun facts that will
tell you all about different places in
Scotland, and Scottish history and wildlife.
Use the stickers at the back of the book
to complete the sticker scenes and your
brightest pens and pencils to complete the
colouring pages. Answers can be found at
the back of the book. Have fun!

GET TO KNOW SCOTLAND

Locate the landmark stickers and fit them into the right spaces on this map of Scotland. Once you know your way around, let's find out more about this magnificent country!

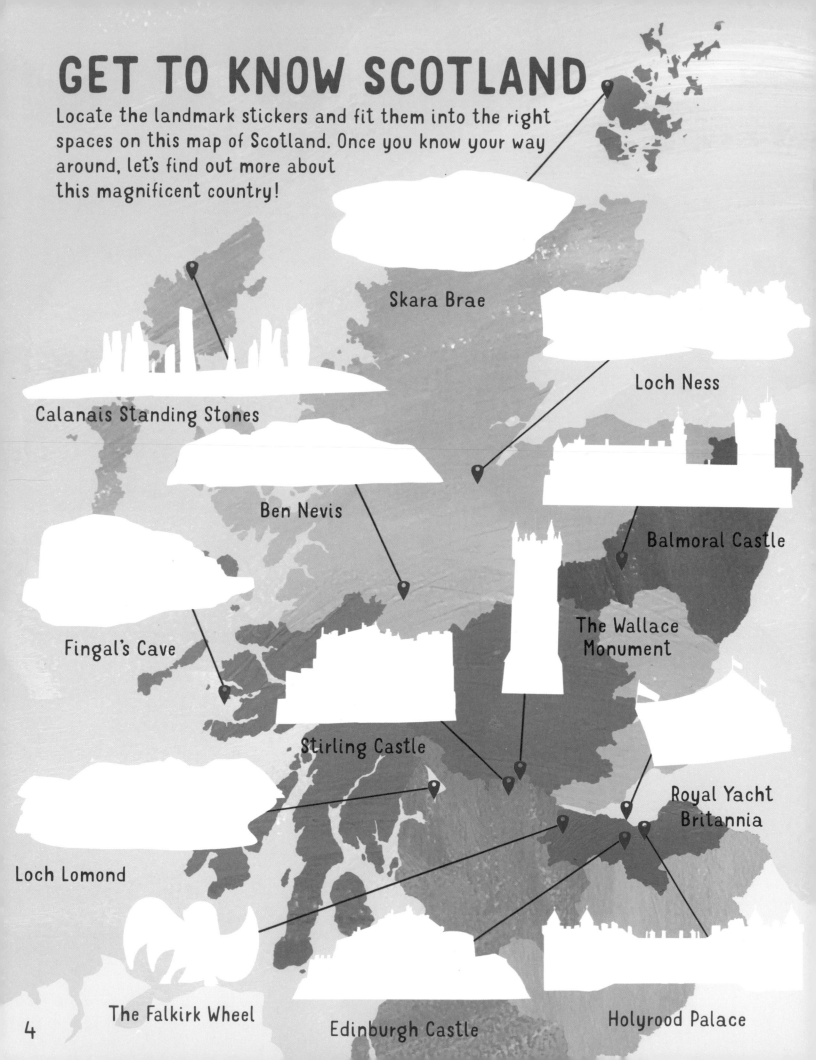

Skara Brae

Loch Ness

Calanais Standing Stones

Ben Nevis

Balmoral Castle

Fingal's Cave

The Wallace Monument

Stirling Castle

Royal Yacht Britannia

Loch Lomond

The Falkirk Wheel

Edinburgh Castle

Holyrood Palace

HIGHLAND WORD SEARCH

How many Highland place names can you find in this word search?

```
X  O  E  I  V  P  Y  T  S  B  S  S  J  L  G
M  C  T  U  R  D  V  L  N  L  A  S  I  L  L
A  N  K  U  D  G  G  R  J  D  G  I  N  I  E
F  K  S  Z  I  T  I  E  M  K  W  E  V  H  N
P  O  R  T  M  A  H  O  M  A  C  K  E  Y  C
D  Y  R  V  N  C  R  N  A  A  W  L  R  T  O
C  I  B  T  O  I  F  Y  P  B  A  P  G  T  E
M  Z  N  N  W  M  G  P  V  D  O  S  O  E  U
S  R  T  G  D  I  L  L  S  N  A  T  R  B  H
Y  I  B  R  W  E  L  M  E  K  D  C  D  W  A
N  B  O  D  C  A  L  L  M  A  S  T  O  W  N
F  A  R  R  N  E  L  S  I  T  E  N  N  U  D
W  Z  O  Y  H  L  D  L  D  A  B  O  Q  K  Z
W  S  S  P  P  E  I  K  R  A  M  E  S  O  R
S  H  A  N  D  W  I  C  K  V  T  W  S  B  T
```

APPLECROSS	DUNNET	GLENCOE	NAIRN
BETTYHILL	ELGIN	HELMSDALE	PORTMAHOMACK
CONTIN	FARR	INVERGORDON	ROSEMARKIE
DINGWALL	FORT WILLIAM	KEISS	SHANDWICK

THE MISSING LETTER MYSTERY

Can you complete these place names with the correct letter tiles? You can only use each letter from the cloud once!

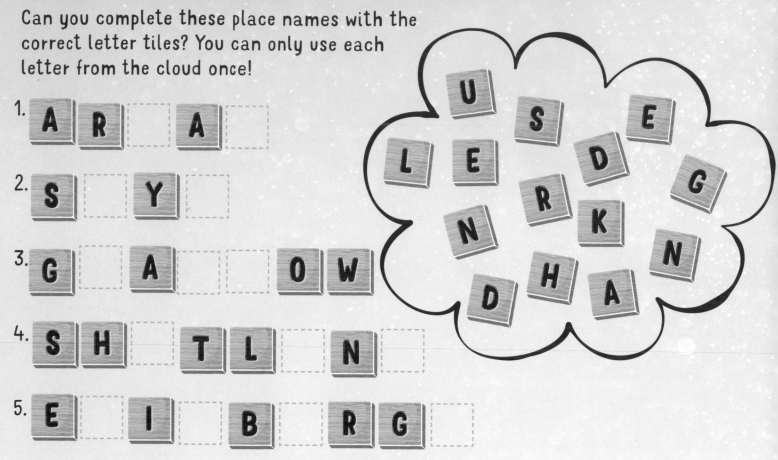

1. A R ☐ A ☐

2. S ☐ ☐ Y ☐

3. G A ☐ A ☐ ☐ O W

4. S H ☐ T L ☐ N ☐

5. E ☐ I ☐ B ☐ R G ☐

Cloud letters: U S E L E D R K N R N H D A G N A

SCOTTISH SYMMETRY

These pictures are symmetrical, which means each side is a mirror image of the other. Fill in the blank side of the picture using what you can see on the other side of the dotted line and match the colours using pens or pencils. Clue: you'll end up with the Flag of Scotland, a thistle and a Scottie dog!

GO PUFFIN-SPOTTING IN SHETLAND

There are lots of puffin colonies to be found on the clifftops around the coast of Scotland and its islands, including Shetland. How many puffins can you count in this scene? Write your answer in the box at the bottom of the page. Now use your stickers to add five more puffins to the scene in all the places you can find space!

SCOTTISH ROYALTY

Colour in these portraits of Mary Queen of Scots and her father, King James V.
Now draw your own king and queen portraits inside the golden frames on the next page. What would you look like if you were wearing a crown?

FUN FACT
When King James V died in 1542, his daughter Mary became the Queen. She was only six days old!

DUNDEE DISCOVERY

The RRS Discovery took Captain Scott and Ernest Shackleton on their first research trip to the South Pole. Constructed in Dundee, this wooden ship was built to survive a journey to the frozen wastes of Antarctica. Colour in the ship and its sails.

DISCOVERY

HIGHLAND DRESS

Use your stickers to clothe these figures in traditional Highland dress.

FUN FACT

Plants, berries and mosses were originally used to dye the wool that was turned into tartan fabric. Each Scottish clan or family would have their own set of colours and patterns for their tartan.

TIME FOR TARTAN

Use these tartan patterns as inspiration to draw and colour some brand new tartan designs. Which one will you choose for your own clan's tartan?

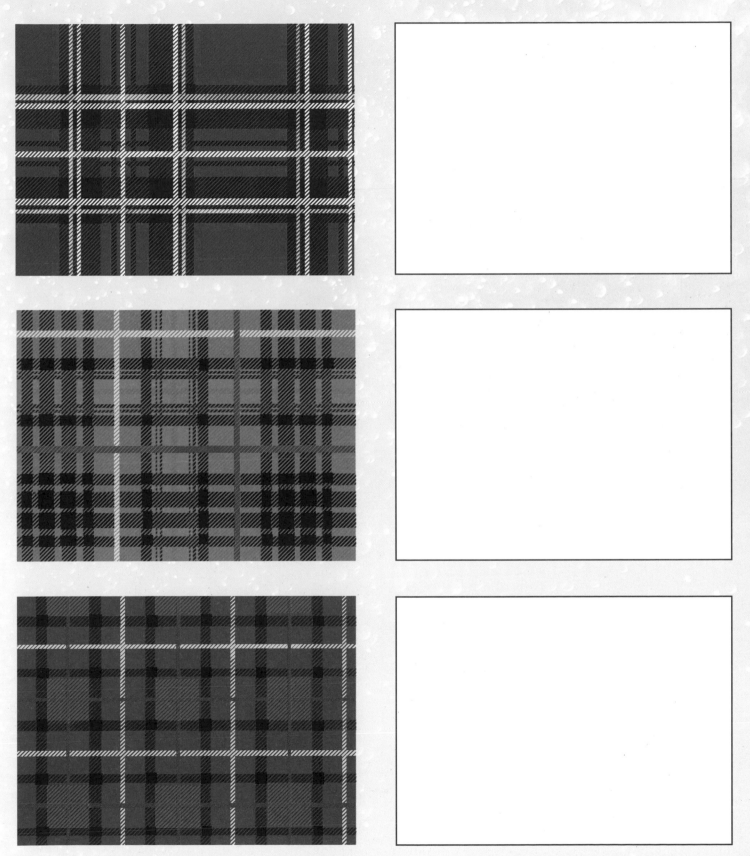

JOHN O'GROATS

John o'Groats is the most northerly point of the British Isles. From here, you can take a ferry to Orkney, go surfing or even spot killer whales out at sea.
Colour in the activities you'd like to take part in if you visited John o'Groats.

JOHN O'GROATS

LANDS END 874m

EDINBURGH 273m

NEW YORK 3230m

ORKNEY 8m   SHETLAND 152m

FUN FACT

The furthest opposite point in the British Isles is called Land's End, which is in Cornwall. It is 874 miles away from John o'Groats and if you journey between these two places, you'll have travelled the whole length of the British Isles!

There are lots of things to do in Aberdeen, including visiting museums and parks. Inside this huge greenhouse in Duthie Park, you'll find all kinds of plants from around the world, including giant cacti and banana trees! Use your stickers to add more plants to the Duthie Park Winter Gardens.

DEER-SPOTTING

Some majestic red deer are hiding in these
Scottish woodlands. How many can you find?
Write your answer in the box.
Were you right?

FAMOUS SCOTS

Do you know why each of these Scots is famous? Draw a line between their name and the achievements on the right-hand side of the page. How many answers did you get right?

Alexander Selkirk

Sir Walter Scott

Katherine Grainger

Sir Alexander Fleming

Sir Chris Hoy

Macbeth

J.M. Barrie

John Logie Baird

Dr David Livingstone

Andy Murray

Olympic cycling champion

Scientist who discovered penicillin

Wrote Peter Pan

Invented the television

Marooned sailor who inspired the book Robinson Crusoe

Olympic rowing champion

Wimbledon tennis champion

Explorer who discovered Victoria Falls in Africa

Author who has a train station named after one of his books

Early King of Scotland

THE FALKIRK WHEEL

The Falkirk Wheel is the world's only rotating boatlift. It lifts boats out of one canal and sets them down in a different one! Look at the picture of the Falkirk Wheel. Can you copy what is in each grid to make an even bigger version? If it's tricky just try the outline then colour it in.

BIKE AROUND THE BORDERS

The Borders is the area of Scotland that sits next to England and is a brilliant place to go mountain biking. Colour in the cyclists using your brightest colours!

How many bicycle wheels can you count in this picture?
Write the number in the box.

LOCH LOMOND

There are all kinds of activities to enjoy on a trip to Loch Lomond! Add tents to the places around the loch to show where you would like to camp. Then stick some kayaks in the water and people fishing along the shore.

Fill your backpack with things you'll need on your camping trip and colour them in!

DESIGN A COAT OF ARMS

Copy colour each of the designs beside the completed one. Now design your own coat of arms in the blank shield.

WALK AROUND EDINBURGH

Take a walking tour around Edinburgh with this city maze. Follow the roads from the start flag to the finish line to make sure you can spot all the sights.

START

EDINBURGH CASTLE

EDINBURGH ZOO

GRASSMARKET

- [ ] Edinburgh Castle
- [ ] The Royal Mile
- [ ] Grassmarket
- [ ] Greyfriars Bobby
- [ ] The Birthplace of Harry Potter
- [ ] National Museum of Scotland
- [ ] Edinburgh Zoo

📍 THE ROYAL MILE

THE BIRTHPLACE OF
HARRY POTTER

📍

GREYFRIARS BOBBY

📍

FINISH

FUN FACT

J.K. Rowling wrote the Harry
Potter books in a cafe near
Edinburgh Castle!

NATIONAL MUSEUM OF SCOTLAND

SPOT ORKNEY VOLES!

Orkney voles are found on the islands of Orkney off the northern coast of Scotland and are twice the size of voles you would see on the mainland! Use your stickers to add some Orkney voles to the island scene once you have counted how many you can see here. Write your answer in the box.

35

HOPPING AROUND THE HEBRIDES

Can you fit each of these Hebridean islands into the grid? Use the letter clues already in place to help you. Each answer can only be used once.

- RUM
- BUTE
- COLL
- EIGG
- IONA
- MULL
- ARRAN
- BARRA
- CANNA
- GIGHA
- ISLAY
- LEWIS
- TIREE
- HARRIS
- CUMBRAE
- ERISKAY
- LISMORE
- BERNERAY
- COLONSAY

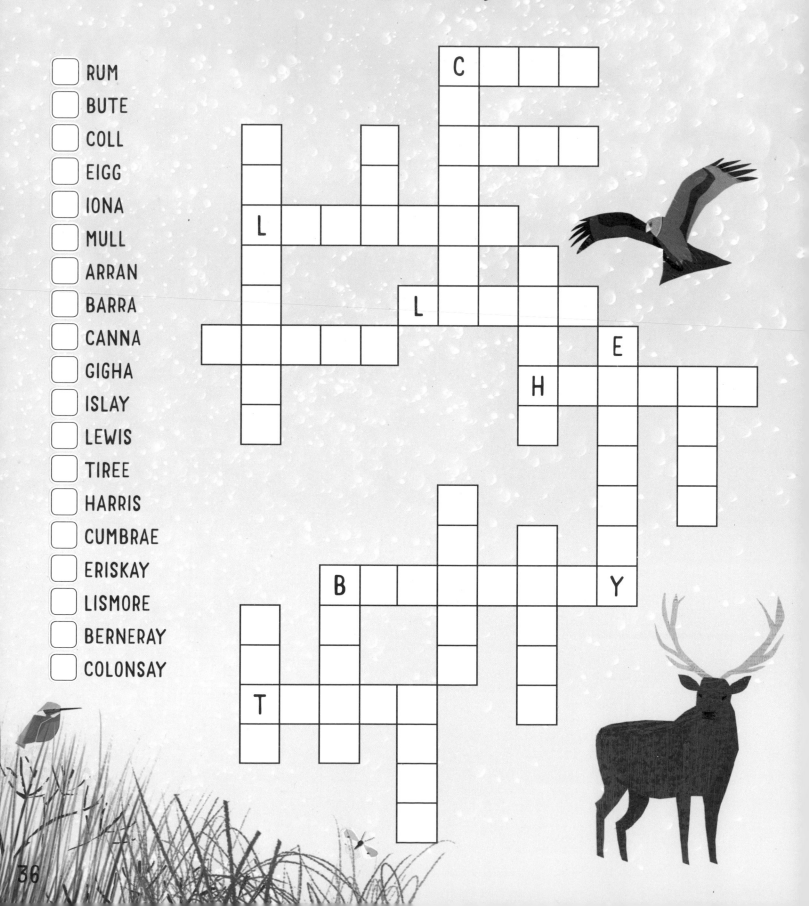

A TRIP TO TOBERMORY

Copy colour these harbour-front houses in the town of Tobermory on the Isle of Mull.

FUN FACT

The BBC children's television programme Balamory was filmed in Tobermory. Children from the local nursery school and the island's fire crew were included in the show!

SALMON-SPOTTING

How many wild salmon can you see
in the rushing river?
Write the answer in the box.

WHAT'S IN THE ROCK POOL?

Add some stickers to this rock pool to show what you might find under the water.

STONE CIRCLES MAZE

Can you find your way out of the stone circles maze?
Start in the centre - good luck!

START

FUN FACT

Just east of Inverness you'll find the Clava Cairns, a group of stone mounds built to honour the dead around 4000 years ago. The cairns are surrounded by stone circles but nobody knows who is buried there or who built them.

FINISH

SCOTTISH NAMES WORD SEARCH

Find the Scottish boys' and girls' names in this word search.

```
P  W  Z  N  H  W  D  W  N  R  Q  C  C  F  D
Y  X  W  W  W  O  C  O  U  E  T  A  A  M  L
H  Y  X  J  U  E  B  C  V  S  U  T  L  L  D
R  X  R  G  A  N  R  O  L  A  Q  R  U  E  T
E  L  L  O  C  J  I  D  C  R  C  I  M  V  C
P  A  F  F  P  R  Y  P  B  N  F  J  O  X  Q  F
S  F  N  O  T  N  P  S  A  A  C  N  J  D  P
K  H  X  S  N  B  E  T  Y  M  J  A  K  W  W
D  W  R  R  B  Q  B  Z  T  M  M  C  L  B  I
J  I  A  G  Z  T  W  D  I  I  O  R  I  B  U
K  Y  B  S  P  A  U  Y  E  B  Y  R  T  T  J
J  H  J  I  D  L  H  A  M  I  S  H  A  E  G
F  C  U  K  J  S  Y  A  L  N  I  F  E  G  Z
P  O  F  F  C  I  P  V  I  B  F  Y  K  Q  E
H  F  F  S  C  P  T  F  L  I  P  Z  J  Z  J
```

FINLAY	RORY	ISLA	CATRIONA
MORAG	FRASER	JAMIE	LORNA
CALUM	KIRSTY	DOUGLAS	
ANDREW	HAMISH		

TIME TO EAT!

Colour in the pictures on this menu of traditional Scottish foods.

Menu

MARMALADE

BREAKFAST

OATCAKES

PORRIDGE

LUNCH

HAGGIS

SCOTCH BROTH

SNACKS

SCOTTISH SALMON

SHORTBREAD

MILK CHOCOLATE
ALLOW·SCOTLAND·MILK CHOCO

TUNNOCK'S
TEACAKES

STICKER FUN

Find the Loch Ness Monster stickers and add them to the water in this lochside scene. Nessie is very shy, so you'll need to be quick if you want to spot her! Add one of your Scottish flag stickers to the castle's flagpole too.

LOCH NESS STORY

Write a story about the Loch Ness Monster here.
Be as creative as you like!

_____

_____

_____

_____

_____

_____

_____

_____

_____

_____

_____

_____

_____

_____

_____

_____

_____

What title will you give to your story?
Draw a cover for a book with this title
and don't forget to add in your name as
the author!

A PALACE IN PERTHSHIRE

Look at the picture of Scone Palace. Can you copy what is in each grid to make an even bigger version to fill the box below?

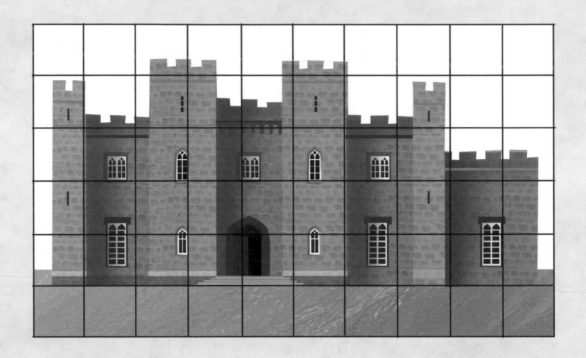

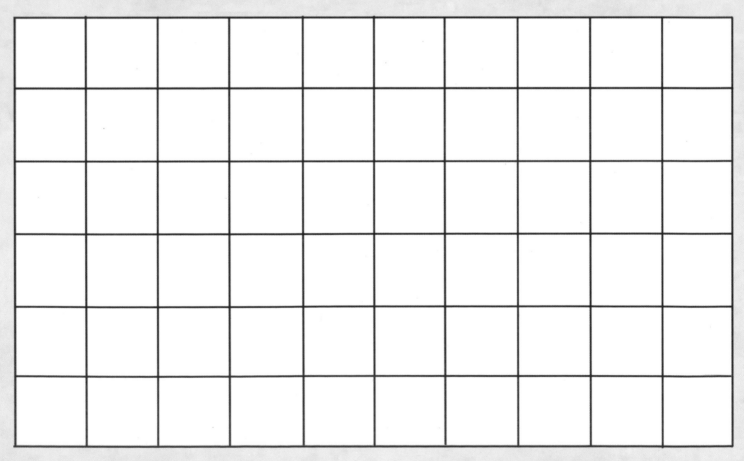

SCOTTISH SPORTS

Can you unscramble the letter tiles to find the names of five Scottish sports?

1. ☐ ☐ L ☐ **O F G**

2. H ☐ G ☐ ☐ ☐ N ☐
   ☐ A ☐ ☐ ☐
   H E D L A M S G I

3. ☐ O ☐ ☐ ☐ A ☐ ☐ **F B O L L T**

4. ☐ U ☐ ☐ ☐ ☐ ☐ **G I N L R C L**

5. ☐ ☐ G ☐ ☐ **Y U R B**

Using just blue and white, create your own Scottish rugby jersey!

KELPIES ...

In Scottish myth, a kelpie is a water spirit which usually takes the shape of a horse. Colour in this picture of a Scottish kelpie and complete it by adding some water splash stickers.

AND SELKIES

A selkie is a mythical creature which takes the form of a seal in the water and a human on land. Colour in this selkie girl, and the seals in the water nearby.

CALANAIS STANDING STONES

The Calanais Standing Stones were put in place over 5000 years ago on the Isle of Lewis in the Outer Hebrides. People come from all around the world to visit the stones, which are older than Stonehenge in England.
In real life the stones are grey, but you can colour these ones however you like!

BESIDE THE FAIRY POOLS

On the Isle of Skye, you'll find a group of sparkling, turquoise pools surrounded by foaming waterfalls. These are known as The Fairy Pools and if you come to see them you'll need to wear waterproof clothing to keep you dry! Use your stickers to dress each of the visitors. Add some red kite birds flying high above the island.

KELVINGROVE MUSEUM

THE TALL SHIP: GLENLEE

THE LIGHTHOUSE

FINISH

GLASGOW SCIENCE CENTRE

- [ ] Ibrox Stadium (Rangers)
- [ ] Celtic Park (Celtic)
- [ ] Glasgow Cathedral and The Necropolis
- [ ] Kelvingrove Museum
- [ ] Glasgow Science Centre
- [ ] The Tall Ship: Glenlee
- [ ] The Lighthouse (Charles Rennie Mackintosh museum)

ALL AROUND GLASGOW

Take a bus tour around Glasgow with this city maze. Follow the roads from the start flag to make sure you tick off each sight you pass before you reach the finish line.

GLASGOW CATHEDRAL AND THE NECROPOLIS

START

CELTIC PARK (CELTIC)

IBROX STADIUM (RANGERS)

58

UNICORN-SPOTTING AT STIRLING CASTLE

The unicorn is one of the symbols of Scotland, and its national animal. Unicorns can be seen all over the country on historic buildings and landmarks. How many unicorns can you find hidden within this picture of Stirling Castle? Write the answer in the box. Colour the sky in your best sunset shades.

Draw a unicorn on this shield.

DOT-TO-DOT DOLPHINS AND SEALS

Can you join the dots to reveal the dolphins and seals that live around the Scottish coastline? Colour them in once they are complete!

61

HAPPY NEW YEAR!

Use your stickers to add Hogmanay fireworks
to the sky over Edinburgh Castle!

ANSWERS

p5. HIGHLAND WORD SEARCH

X	O	E	I	V	P	Y	T	S	B	S	S	J	L	G
M	C	T	U	R	D	V	L	N	L	A	S	I	L	L
A	N	K	U	D	G	G	R	J	D	G	I	N	I	E
F	K	S	Z	I	T	I	E	M	K	W	E	V	H	N
P	O	R	T	M	A	H	O	M	A	C	K	E	Y	C
D	Y	R	V	N	C	R	N	A	A	W	L	R	T	O
C	I	B	T	O	I	F	Y	P	B	A	P	G	T	E
M	Z	N	N	W	M	G	P	V	D	O	S	O	E	U
S	R	T	G	D	I	L	L	S	N	A	T	R	B	H
Y	I	B	R	W	E	L	M	E	K	D	C	D	W	A
N	B	O	D	C	A	L	L	M	A	S	T	O	W	N
F	A	R	R	N	E	L	S	I	T	E	N	N	U	D
W	Z	O	Y	H	L	D	L	D	A	B	O	Q	K	Z
W	S	S	P	P	E	I	K	R	A	M	E	S	O	R
S	H	A	N	D	W	I	C	K	V	T	W	S	B	T

p6. THE MISSING LETTER MYSTERY
1. Arran 2. Skye 3. Glasgow
4. Shetland 5. Edinburgh

p9. SKIING IN THE CAIRNGORMS
1-E, 2-C, 3-B, 4-A, 5-D

p10. GO PUFFIN-SPOTTING IN SHETLAND
22 Puffins

p22. DEER-SPOTTING
16 Deer

p24. FAMOUS SCOTS
Alexander Selkirk – Marooned sailor
Sir Walter Scott – Author
Katherine Grainger – Olympic rowing champion
Sir Alexander Fleming – Scientist
Sir Chris Hoy – Olympic cycling champion
Macbeth – Early King of Scotland
J.M. Barrie – Wrote Peter Pan
John Logie Baird – Invented the television
Dr David Livingstone – Explorer
Andy Murray – Wimbledon tennis champion

p26. BIKE AROUND THE BORDERS
9 Wheels

p34. SPOT ORKNEY VOLES!
18 Voles

p36. HOPPING AROUND THE HEBRIDES

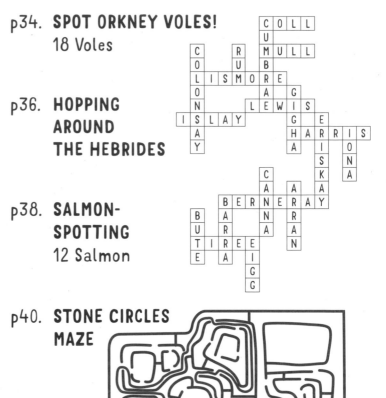

p38. SALMON-SPOTTING
12 Salmon

p40. STONE CIRCLES MAZE

p42. SCOTTISH NAMES WORD SEARCH

P	W	Z	N	H	W	D	W	N	R	Q	C	C	F	D
Y	X	W	W	W	O	C	O	U	E	T	A	A	M	L
H	Y	X	J	U	E	B	C	V	S	U	T	L	L	D
R	X	R	G	A	N	R	O	L	A	Q	R	U	E	T
E	L	L	O	C	J	I	D	C	R	C	I	M	V	C
P	A	F	P	R	Y	P	B	N	F	J	O	X	Q	F
S	F	N	O	T	N	P	S	A	A	C	N	J	D	P
K	H	X	S	N	B	E	T	Y	M	J	A	K	W	W
D	W	R	R	B	Q	B	Z	T	M	M	C	L	B	I
J	I	A	G	Z	T	W	D	I	I	O	R	I	B	U
K	Y	B	S	P	A	U	Y	E	B	Y	R	T	T	J
J	H	J	I	D	L	H	A	M	I	S	H	A	E	G
F	C	U	K	J	S	Y	A	L	N	I	F	E	G	Z
P	O	F	F	C	I	P	V	I	B	F	Y	K	Q	E
H	F	F	S	C	P	T	F	L	I	P	Z	J	Z	J

p49. SCOTTISH SPORTS
1. Golf 2. Highland Games
3. Football 4. Curling 5. Rugby

p58. UNICORN-SPOTTING AT STIRLING CASTLE
16 Unicorns